P9-DEG-822

I Am in Charge of Me

Read-It! Readers
Red Level

By Dana Meachen Rau

Illustrated by Shirley Beckes

Special thanks to our advisers for their expertise:

Adria F. Klein, Ph.D.
Professor Emeritus, California State University
San Bernardino, California

Rosemary G. Palmer, Ph.D.
Department of Literacy, College of Education
Boise State University

Levels for *Read-it!* Readers

- Familiar topics
- Frequently used words
- Repeating patterns

- New ideas
- Larger vocabulary
- Variety of language structures

- Challenges in ideas
- Expanded vocabulary
- Wide variety of sentences

- More complex ideas
- Extended vocabulary range
- Expanded language structures

A Note to Parents and Caregivers:

Read-it! Readers are for children who are just starting on the amazing road to reading. These beautiful books support both the acquisition of reading skills and the love of books.

The RED LEVEL presents familiar topics using common words and repeating sentence patterns.

The BLUE LEVEL presents new ideas using a larger vocabulary and varied sentence structure.

The YELLOW LEVEL presents more challenging ideas, a broad vocabulary, and wide variety in sentence structure.

The GREEN LEVEL presents more complex ideas, an extended vocabulary range, and expanded language structures.

When sharing a book with your child, read in short stretches, pausing often to talk about the pictures. Have your child turn the pages and point to the pictures and familiar words. And be sure to reread favorite stories or parts of stories.

There is no right or wrong way to share books with children. Find time to read with your child, and pass on the legacy of literacy.

Adria F. Klein, Ph.D.
Professor Emeritus
California State University
San Bernardino, California

Managing Editor: Catherine Neitge
Creative Director: Terri Foley
Editor: Patricia Stockland
Designer: Jaime Martens
Page production: Picture Window Books
The illustrations in this book were prepared digitally.

Picture Window Books
5115 Excelsior Boulevard
Suite 232
Minneapolis, MN 55416
877-845-8392
www.picturewindowbooks.com

Printed in the United States of America.

Library of Congress Cataloging-in-Publication Data
Rau, Dana Meachen, 1971-
I am in charge of me / by Dana Meachen Rau ; illustrated by Shirley Beckes.
p. cm. — (Read-it! readers)
Summary: A boy recounts the many things in his life that he is responsible for.
ISBN 1-4048-0646-6 (hardcover)
[1. Responsibility—Fiction. 2. Self-perception—Fiction. 3. Self-confidence—Fiction.]
I. Beckes, Shirley V., ill. II. Title. III. Series.
PZ7.R193975Iae 2004
[E]—dc22 2004007360

I am in charge of me!

I am in charge of my clothes.

I am in charge of my bed.

I am in charge of my backpack.

I am in charge of the lunch line.

LUNCHROOM

I am in charge of my books.

QUIET
PLEASE

I am in charge of my mittens.

I am in charge of my sled.

I am in charge of my coat.

I am in charge
of my fish.

I am in charge of the table.

I am in charge of my teeth.

I am in charge of my toys.

I am in charge of me!

Levels for *Read-it!* Readers

Read-it! Readers help children practice early reading skills with brightly illustrated stories.

Red Level: Familiar topics with frequently used words and repeating patterns.

I Am in Charge of Me by Dana Meachen Rau
Let's Share by Dana Meachen Rau

Blue Level: New ideas with a larger vocabulary and a variety of language structures.

At the Beach by Patricia M. Stockland
The Playground Snake by Brian Moses

Yellow Level: Challenging ideas with an expanded vocabulary and a wide variety of sentences.

Flynn Flies High by Hilary Robinson
Marvin, the Blue Pig by Karen Wallace
Moo! by Penny Dolan
Pippin's Big Jump by Hilary Robinson
The Queen's Dragon by Anne Cassidy
Sounds Like Fun by Dana Meachen Rau
Tired of Waiting by Dana Meachen Rau
Whose Birthday Is It? by Sherryl Clark

Green Level: More complex ideas with an extended vocabulary range and expanded language structures.

Clever Cat by Karen Wallace
Flora McQuack by Penny Dolan
Izzie's Idea by Jillian Powell
Naughty Nancy by Anne Cassidy
The Princess and the Frog by Margaret Nash
The Roly-Poly Rice Ball by Penny Dolan
Run! by Sue Ferraby
Sausages! by Anne Adeney
Stickers, Shells, and Snow Globes by Dana Meachen Rau
The Truth About Hansel and Gretel by Karina Law
Willie the Whale by Joy Oades

A complete list of _Read-it!_ Readers is available on our Web site: www.picturewindowbooks.com